Helen Paiba was one of the most committed, knowledgeable and acclaimed children's booksellers in Britain. For more than twenty years she owned and ran the Children's Bookshop in Muswell Hill, London, which under her guidance gained a superb reputation for its range of children's books and for the advice available to its customers.

Helen was also involved with the Booksellers Association for many years and served on both its Children's Bookselling Group and the Trade Practices Committee.

In 1995 she was given honorary life membership of the Booksellers Association of Great Britain and Ireland in recognition of her outstanding services to the association and to the book trade. In the same year the Children's Book Circle (sponsored by Books for Children) honoured her with the Eleanor Farjeon Award, given for distinguished service to the world of children's books.

Books in this series

Bedtime stories

for **6** year olds

Chosen by Helen Paiba

Illustrated by Annabel Hudson

MACMILLAN CHILDREN'S BOOKS

First published 2001 by Macmillan Children's Books

This edition published 2017 by Macmillan Children's Books
an imprint of Pan Macmillan
20 New Wharf Road, London N1 9RR
Associated companies throughout the world
www.panmacmillan.com

ISBN 978-1-5098-3887-5

Typeset by SX Composing DTP, Rayleigh, Essex
Printed and bound by CPI Group (UK) Ltd, Croydon CR0 4YY

Contents

The Pretend Pony

Barbee Oliver Carleton

There once was a boy named Pee-wee who wanted a pony so much that he could think of nothing else. "Come to supper!" his mother would call.

Pee-wee washed his hands and sat down at the table nicely enough. But right away he started thinking about that pony. Soon his supper was stone-cold, and everybody else was finished.

"Bedtime, Pee-wee," his father would say. Pee-wee started off well enough by cleaning his teeth and scrubbing his ears. But sooner or later he began thinking about the pony. There they would find him in the morning, sound asleep on the rug, with his clothes still on and a wishful smile on his face.

"Something has to be done about that pony," said Pee-wee's mother.

"But not this year," said Father.

So they shook their heads and did nothing about the pony at all.

Soon Pee-wee's jolly Uncle Wally came to visit. When he saw that the pony was all Pee-wee could think about, he said, "Pee-wee, you

2

just PRETEND you have that pony. If you pretend a thing hard enough, sometimes it comes true."

Pee-wee grew excited for the first time in weeks. "How long will it take?" he cried.

Jolly Uncle Wally scratched his head. "Oh, I should say maybe three days."

"Now, Wally," said Pee-wee's mother.

But Pee-wee got right to work. First of all, he had to have a pony shed. The old woodshed would do, Pee-wee decided. All that first morning he worked. He cleaned out the shed and swept it carefully. He nailed down planks to mend

3

the floor. He tacked tarred paper on to the roof to keep the pony dry. And all the time he worked, Pee-wee pretended hard that the pony was just outside, grazing in the grass.

When they called him to supper, Pee-wee rode fast across the field

2

on the pretend pony. He reached the house a great deal sooner than ever before.

"How strange!" said Pee-wee's mother, watching at the window. "Pee-wee seems to be several feet off the ground!"

"So he does," said Father, peering. "That boy is pretending that pony so hard, I can almost see it myself!"

Jolly Uncle Wally just puffed on his pipe.

That was the first day.

On the second day, Pee-wee built the pony stall. For the walls, he used some old planks that were out behind the shed. After that, he built a fine feed bin, just as high as a pony's nose. Next he built a shelf to hold the water pail. And all day long, as hard as he worked, Pee-wee pretended even harder. He pretended that his pony was grazing just outside the shed, and that he was brown with maybe a white star on his soft nose.

When they called him to supper, Pee-wee untied the pretend pony. He clucked his tongue and galloped to the house in less time than it takes to tell about it.

Father blinked his eyes. "I must need glasses very badly," he said. "Pee-wee seems to be several feet off the ground again."

"Not only that," whispered Pee-wee's mother. "He appears to be mounted on SOMETHING BROWN!"

Pee-wee tied the pretend pony to the porch rail and came in, not one bit out of breath. Jolly Uncle Wally gave Pee-wee a broad wink, and kept on puffing his pipe.

That was the second day.

On the third and last day, Pee-wee worked hard to put up a fence. All that morning, jolly Uncle Wally helped him. But he had to go away for a while, so Pee-wee finished the fence by himself. Last of all, he filled the pony's water pail and fed him.

7

But not for a minute did Pee-wee forget to pretend. He pretended that the brown pony with the white star on his nose was just outside, grazing in the field. He even pretended that his brown pony had a golden tan cowboy saddle with a new rope coiled on the pommel. He pretended harder than ever before. He pretended so hard that his hair felt tight around his head.

When they called him to supper, Pee-wee went outside the shed. Sure enough, just as jolly Uncle Wally had said, the pony had come true! He was soft brown, with a white star on his nose, and he wore a golden tan cowboy saddle with a new rope coiled on the pommel. Pee-wee stroked the pony's neck. His coat was soft and his breath was warm and sweet.

Pee-wee's mother and father looked out of the window and their eyes grew very round. "A brown pony with a saddle," Mother whispered. "I never would have believed it!"

Father shook his head. "I still don't," he said.

Jolly Uncle Wally walked across the field, puffing on his pipe. Proudly, Pee-wee rode up to him. "Looks as though I pretended

hard enough, doesn't it?" he said.
"Looks that way," smiled Uncle
Wally.

Elephant Milk, Hippopotamus Cheese

Margaret Mahy

There was once an orphan named Deedee who had the biggest feet in the world. They were so big she had grown extra strong ankles and knees in order to pick them up and put them down again. These enormous feet were a great embarrassment to her, and to the matron of the

11

orphanage, as well. She didn't like having such a big-footed orphan clumping around her. She thought it spoiled the look of the orphanage.

Now, just down the road, there lived a man and a woman who were so lazy they had not washed the dishes for three years. Dirty dishes were piled up to the kitchen ceiling, down the hall, and along the driveway. It was lucky for them they had been given so many cups, saucers, and plates when they were married. However, one morning, they got up and looked around and found they had run out of clean dishes.

"What *shall* we do?" cried the man. "We positively can't wash all these, and yet there isn't a clean dish in the house."

"Phone up the orphanage," suggested his wife, "and we'll adopt a daughter to wash our dishes for us. Then, when she's done, we'll eat clean again."

"What a good idea!" cried the man, and he called the orphanage at once.

"Have you got a girl orphan who can cook and clean all day, and half the night as well?" he asked. "I don't want one that needs a lot of food or sleep, but I want one that's a good, strong, steady girl, because there's a lot to do around here, and my wife and I are very delicate."

"Yes, yes," said the orphanage matron. "We have just the orphan for you. Her name is Weedy Deedee. She won't eat much. She's little and thin, but she's got such big feet she's as steady as a rock. I'll send her round in a brace of shakes." Then she went to the window and called, "Deedee! Deedee! Weedy Deedee! Pack your bag and sign the book. You've been adopted by the people down the road."

Weedy Deedee came clumping down the road from the

orphanage, her big feet looking particularly enormous in their blue sneakers. She was about as tall as a rosebush, thin as string, with hair like bootlaces, and feet like rowboats, but she had gentle, hopeful eyes and a lovely smile.

When she saw the dishes all the

way down the driveway she sighed and set to work. She washed cups and saucers, bread and butter plates, dinner plates, soup bowls, salad bowls, mugs, glasses, and tankards. She rinsed knives and forks and spoons, and then scoured saucepans, soup-pots, and skillets. She washed dishes all the way up the driveway, all the way down the hall, and all the way through the kitchen from floor to ceiling. Finally, every dish was clean and every spoon sparkling.

"What next?" asked Weedy Deedee for she knew there was more to come.

"Dear adopted daughter

Deedee," said the man. "You may do the washing."

"And then the ironing!" said his wife.

"Make the beds!" commanded the man.

"Polish the furniture!" cried the woman.

"Chase the spiders!"

"Swat the flies!"

"Sweep!"

"Dust!"

"And then when you've done that, you may weed the flowerbeds," the man concluded.

It looks like a full morning, thought Weedy Deedee. So she set to work. Though she was little and stringy she was strong at heart. She washed and ironed, made and polished, chased and swatted, and swept, dusted, and weeded. The house shone like a treasure as much to be looked at as lived in.

"That's that!" said Weedy Deedee. "And now, dear adopted parents, may I please have something to eat because I'm very hungry, and it's a long way past my dinner time."

The man and the woman looked at each other in dismay. They hadn't reckoned on feeding her.

"She's very small," said the man doubtfully.

"Except for her feet!" the woman

muttered. "I've heard that those with extra large feet eat extra large dinners in order to maintain them."

"And she's worked very hard too. She must be tremendously hungry by now," the man said. "Never mind! I have an idea. Leave this to me." Then he turned to Deedee. "Dear adopted daughter," he said, "we have a delicious meal of roast turkey and cranberry sauce, not to mention three colours of jelly and ice cream for dessert. But your dear adopted mother and I have one more job for you. We want you to paint the ceiling."

"It certainly needs it," said

Deedee. "Where's the ladder?"

"That's the problem. We don't have a ladder," said the man with a horrid smile.

"Then I'll stand on the table," Deedee said.

"What!" cried the woman. "Stand on my beautiful, polished, mahogany table with your whopping great feet? Never!"

"But I can't reach the ceiling!" exclaimed Deedee. "I'm too small."

"Oh, dear," the man said, shaking his head. "So you are. How tragic. You'd better go back to the orphanage until you've grown taller. How sad. It breaks our hearts. And you've done so well too, up to now."

"That's it," cried the woman. "Come back when you're taller."

"You're still our dear adopted daughter, and we'll think of you fondly and pray for the day that you grow about three feet further towards the ceiling."

Weedy Deedee hadn't unpacked yet. She clumped all the way back to the orphanage with her change of clothes and her toothbrush in a small case. But when she got there, the gate was closed tight.

"Off you go!" said the matron, popping her head out of the window. "We got another orphan in the moment you left, and there isn't any room now for you."

"What shall I do?" asked Weedy Deedee.

"Anything you like!" said the matron. "You're as free as a bird. Ah, freedom . . . freedom . . . would that I were as free and as happy-go-lucky as you!" and she popped her head back in again and locked the window . . . just to make sure.

So Weedy Deedee was turned loose on the world to wander and wonder. The roads of the world were very dusty and long, but luckily at that time of the year they were very pretty, all tangled along the sides with buttercups, daisies, and foxgloves. She wandered and she wondered for quite a long time, until even *her* feet became sore and tired, in spite of being big. So when she came to a clear stream, its banks all tall with foxgloves, Weedy Deedee sat down on the bank, took off her blue sneakers, and put her feet into the water where they floated like two great white fish among the reeds.

"Oh, I'm so *hungry*," sighed Weedy Deedee. "I could eat a whole fried elephant and still have room for a hippopotamus in chocolate sauce for dessert."

Funnily enough, just as she said this, an elephant came around the corner of the road, and then another and another, until there was a whole herd of elephants eating up the buttercups and daisies. Then a hippopotamus came around the corner, and another and another, until a whole herd of hippos was waddling by, all smiling and beguiling in the afternoon sunshine.

Then came a different sound of feet, really big feet this time, feet that were certainly even bigger than Weedy Deedee's. She could hear them coming down the road and around the corner, and the thought of bigger feet than hers so terrified her that she jumped up

and tried to hide in a clump of
foxgloves. She was so weedy she
fitted in among the foxgloves
easily . . . all except her feet, of
course. They, poor lonely things
that they were, had to stay
sticking out into the world where
everyone could see them.

Suddenly the herdsman – owner
of the herds of elephants and
hippos – came around the corner.
He was definitely a giant, young
and probably very handsome,
except he was so big it was
difficult to take him in all at once.
By the time you got to his nose,
you had forgotten what his
eyebrows were like. He had a lion

bounding beside him, a kind of working dog. He saw Weedy Deedee's sneakers looking like blue canoes moored among the buttercups and daisies on the bank of the stream.

"What beautiful shoes!" he cried wistfully. "Oh, if I were to find the feet that fitted this footwear I know I would love them." Weedy Deedee couldn't help wiggling her toes through sheer nervousness and the movement caught the giant's blue eyes.

"What beautiful feet sticking out of the foxgloves," he exclaimed in amazement. "What rounded rosy heels, what wonderful wiggling toes! If I could meet the maiden attached to these adorable extremities, I would make her mine. These must be the most beautiful feet in the whole world."

Weedy Deedee couldn't help laughing.

"They're the biggest, anyway!" she cried, looking out through the foxgloves.

The giant stared at her in astonishment. Then he began to laugh too. The lion licked Weedy Deedee's feet and made them tickle, so that the laughing went on for some time.

"Well, that's life!" said the giant at last. "I find a pair of feet to love and they're attached to Deedee, who is no bigger than a rose bush. Never mind! Come out of the foxgloves, for there's no need to hide. The lion's tame and so am I. The elephants and the hippos can wallow and graze, and you can sit and share my lunch with me."

"That would be wonderful," said Weedy Deedee, "because I've had a really full day so far. I was adopted first thing this morning, then I washed three years' worth of dirty dishes, and cleaned a very messy house. Then it turned out I wasn't tall enough to paint the ceiling, and I had to go back to the orphanage until I grew three feet taller. But, meanwhile, the orphanage had got another orphan in my place so I was set free as a bird, and I wandered and wondered my way here. I'm as hungry as a hippopotamus, for I haven't had a bite or sup all day."

"It doesn't bear thinking of," said the giant and passed her a slice of cheese as big as a tray and a cup of milk as large as a bucket, while his elephants grazed around eating the buttercups and daisies, and the hippos had a nice wet wallow under the willow trees.

A strange thing happened. As Weedy Deedee ate the cheese and drank the milk she thought that

29

her feet had suddenly grown smaller.

"Look at that!" she cried. "My feet have suddenly gone all little. What a pity! Up till now my feet were the only bit of me that anyone has ever admired."

"They haven't got smaller," said the giant. "It's you who've grown taller. It must be from drinking elephant milk and eating hippopotamus cheese. After all, that's what I've eaten all my life, and look at me. You've actually grown about three feet taller."

"What?" cried Weedy Deedee. "Do you mean that I've grown tall enough to paint the ceiling . . . just when I was enjoying myself?"

"Oh, forget about that!" said the giant. "Stay here and grow even taller and marry me. I've got a castle up on the hill with a garden full of sunflowers. Be mine and we will herd elephants and hippos together and garden, and have forty-nine children – seven times seven – and live happily ever after."

Now she was a bit bigger, and could take in rather more of the giant's enormous face, Weedy Deedee could see he had a nose she liked and trusted.

"That sounds like a wonderful life," she said. "But I'd better paint the ceiling first, and tell my parents that I'm getting married. After all they did adopt me this morning, and my mother might like to help me make my wedding dress. I've read that that's what mothers do. I'll go home, paint the ceiling, and get the wedding dress, and then I'll come back to you."

"Take some milk and cheese to eat on the way," said the giant. "I've plenty left."

So Deedee put some milk and cheese into a bundle, put on her blue sneakers, and set off over the roads of the world, golden in the evening sunlight.

The man and the woman who

had adopted her were eating a dinner of roast turkey and cranberry sauce. Three colours of jelly, as well as ice cream, stood waiting for their attention. Dirty breakfast and lunch dishes were piled on the clean bench. Deedee looked at them sternly.

"It's our darling adopted daughter back again so soon," said the man uneasily.

"And she's grown!" remarked the woman sourly. "She *has* grown. She's grown enough to paint the ceiling, after all. It shows what you can do if you put your mind to it."

"The paint pots are in the wash

house," the man said.

Deedee mixed the paint and cleaned the brushes. Without any trouble at all, she painted the ceiling, while the man and the woman watched her, throwing the turkey bones over their shoulders.

"Dear adopted mother," said Deedee while she painted. "I am going to be married, and I thought you might help me make my wedding dress."

"Me!" screeched the woman. "Me make a wedding dress for a weedy, not-so-little Deedee who I've only just met today. Think again!"

Deedee did think again and

looked very seriously at her darling adopted mother.

The man smiled at her weakly. "Have a wing of turkey!" he said. "Only a wing! There isn't a lot of meat on a turkey and my wife and I – we're very delicate, you know, and the doctor said . . ."

"Thank you! I've brought my own supper," Deedee replied, and she poured her elephant milk into a tall vase and put her hippopotamus cheese on a platter before her.

"What's that?" asked her adopted parents greedily.

"Elephant milk and hippopotamus cheese," Deedee

told them, and she drank every drop and ate every crumb.

Suddenly her feet looked a lot smaller and the ceiling a lot closer. Weedy Deedee was weedy no more. She grew up through the house. Her arms went out through the windows, her head burst through the ceiling. Stretching towards the sky, she felt the whole house lift off its floor and fold around her a wedding dress of wood and tin, shining with polish and paint.

Down below on the floor, the man and the woman sat among their great set of dishes, dirty and clean, staring at her with terror.

Weedy Deedee had grown, at last, to match her feet.

"Get your great feet out of here!" shouted the man, sounding as whining as a spiteful gnat. "Get out, get out, you diabolical Deedee!"

"I'm going! I'm taking my feet where they will be well and truly appreciated," Deedee replied calmly. "And don't call me Deedee any more. Call me . . . Désirée."

Back up the road went Deedee-Désirée wearing the wedding-dress house, until the roads of the world led her to the giant's castle. The giant came down through the sunflowers to meet her, his faithful lion bounding at his side.

"I was waiting for you," he said. "What took you so long?"

"Painting the ceiling!" said Deedee-Désirée with a laugh. "This is the only wedding dress in the world with a painted ceiling."

So they were married, and together they washed dishes and weeded gardens, herded hippos and milked elephants. They had seven times seven (forty-nine) children who played among the sunflowers. And these children grew to be the most beautiful and happy giants in the land, with bright eyes and the nicest feet in the world – and so they should

have been, for they lived on elephant milk and hippopotamus cheese, and a handful of sunflower seeds whenever they felt like a change.

A Zebra for Helen

A patchwork quilt story

Adèle Geras

Aunt Pinny sat at the foot of my bed, gently stroking a small patch of black-and-white striped material.

"Why are you stroking that?" I asked.

"Because it reminds me of Helen. She was my first real friend, and these stripes remind me of the day I first met her. Shall

I tell you about it?"

"Yes, please," I said, and pulled the quilt up round my shoulders.

"Helen comes into the story at the end, although, as you shall see, she's very important. It all began a few weeks before Christmas. I was six years old. My mother was spending every spare moment cutting, stitching and stuffing soft toys. They were not for me. They were to be sold at the Christmas jumble sale in our Church Hall, to raise money for a nearby orphanage. I longed for some of them, though. There were velvet rabbits, elephants with silken ears, and a chicken trimmed with real feathers. There was a plush cat with huge, gold buttons for eyes and a tiny felt mouth. There was even a lion with real woollen strands standing out round his head. I said to my mother, 'Why don't you ever make animals like these for me?'

" 'Because, child, I have our living to earn. My dresses would never be finished if I spent all my time on toys.'

" 'But you're spending all your time on toys now,' I muttered, near to tears.

"My mother put down the satin snake she was sewing. 'Darling, that's for charity. And besides, you know Miss Snow. It's very hard to say "no" to such a lady!'

"That was true. Miss Snow, our vicar's sister, was a solid mountain of a woman, tightly squeezed into grey dresses so stiff they seemed to be made of metal. She had hard blue eyes like marbles, and smiling was something she almost never did.

" 'If you like, I'll cut you out a pattern,' my mother went on, 'and you can sew your own little animal.' She looked through the basket of materials on the sofa beside her. 'How about this? We could make a small zebra.' She held out a piece of black-and-white striped cotton.

" 'Can't I make a velvet rabbit instead?' I asked her.

" 'I'm afraid not, Pinny dear. Miss Snow asked for a great many rabbits. It seems they are very popular with the children, and I haven't very much velvet left. I'm sorry.'

"I could see it was no use at all. I felt angry and miserable, and determined not to take the least bit of trouble over the zebra. I nearly said I didn't want to make one at all, but I was bored and my mother was busy, so I thought I might just as well sew as do anything else. 'I'll try a zebra, then. Will you cut it out for me, please.'

"To watch my mother cut something out was a treat. Snip went the silver scissors and there was an ear, snap and there was a leg, snip, snap, snip and there were two identical zebra-shaped pieces lying on the carpet, so life-like that they almost seemed to be prancing away on their tiny hooves. I began to like the zebra a little.

" 'Now you must sew all round the edges, dear, neatly, mind you, and leave the tummy open for the stuffing. We'll sew it up at the end.'

"I sat on a stool beside my

46

mother and sewed as neatly as I could. I pricked my finger once, in spite of my thimble, and a little drop of blood fell on the material. I rubbed it off at once, but it left a mark. I tried to sew over the stain, but a little bit still showed. I thought: I don't care. It'll be a rotten old zebra, anyway. I stitched and stitched and, after a while, my zebra was ready to be stuffed. I showed it to my mother.

" 'That's lovely, dear,' she said, but she didn't mean it. It was just that she didn't want to hurt my feelings. I thought that maybe it would look better when it had been stuffed, and I said so. My

mother looked relieved. 'Oh, I'm
sure it will. Let's stuff it at once.'

"We pushed small pieces of rag
into the gaping stomach, and
sewed it up. I sewed on two black
buttons for eyes, and my mother
embroidered a red mouth, and
then we looked at it, standing
lopsided on the carpet. I burst into
tears.

" 'Pinny, love, what's the matter?
There's your lovely zebra that you
made yourself. You should be
proud. Why ever are you crying?'

" 'When you cut it out it was
really a zebra, small and prancing
and so pretty, but now I've sewn it,
it's lumpy and its back is crooked,

and its ears aren't the right shape
and it can hardly stand, and it's
got a spot of my blood on it. I don't
like it, and I don't want to keep
it.'"

"In the end, my mother calmed
me down with a cup of warm milk,
and the promise of a whole
sixpence to spend at the jumble

sale, on whatever I liked. I went to bed that night and dreamed of my crooked zebra, unable to run through the grass with his real zebra friends.

"Next morning, I gave the zebra to my mother for the Soft Toy Stall, and she was very pleased. 'If you don't want it, I'm sure there's some child who will. Thank you, Pinny. I shall tell Miss Snow that it's your contribution, and I shall put it right at the front of the stall.'

"I spent the next few days thinking about how I would spend my money. On the day of the jumble sale, my mother wrapped the sixpence in tissue paper, and put it into my pocket. I felt it with my fingers every few minutes as we walked to the Church Hall, just to make certain it was still there, safe.

"The Church Hall looked splendid. Usually, it was a brown and green box with a dusty stage at the far end, full of little draughts of wind that puffed around your feet. But now it was decorated with holly wreaths and red ribbons and paper lanterns, and filled with stalls full of treasures. I didn't know where to look first, and I was standing in the doorway deciding where to go,

51

when Miss Snow, in a shiny, steel dress (shiny, because this was an occasion) pushed her way between the stalls towards us. She ignored me completely, but she said to my mother: 'Ah, capital, Mrs Pintle. All ready for the fray, I see. Good, good. The public will be arriving in half an hour. Would you be so good as to put the finishing touches to your stall? Thank you so much.'

"She gathered her skirts together and ploughed back to where she came from. My mother hurried away. I looked around. Ladies behind each stall were arranging, rearranging, counting

out piles of pennies, smoothing
their hair, smiling, fluttering
fingers to their brooches, waving
to one another. One other person
was standing about, like me, and
that was the vicar. He was a small,
mouse-like man, with soft, white
hands and soft, white hair. He
came and spoke to me for a while,
about how lovely the Hall looked,
and how hard everyone had
worked, and about what I was
going to buy, until Miss Snow
towed him away to help sort out
the second-hand books. I was left
alone to look at everything.

"Some stalls I didn't even stop at.
I wasn't interested in pots of

home-made jam, or ugly vases, or second-hand baby clothes. I didn't need lace mats, or unpolished brass candlesticks, or pin cushions. My mother's stall was the best. It would have looked like a whole zoo of wonderful animals, if it were not for my zebra right in the front row. I looked at him for a long time. It seemed to me as though the other animals were staring at him out of their button eyes, as if to say: 'Whatever are *you* doing here? You should go somewhere else. We are beautiful beasts, while you are not beautiful at all.' I was surprised to find myself feeling cross with the other soft toys. I even turned one particularly smug tiger right round, because he was looking so pleased with himself that I didn't want to see his face. I said to the zebra, in a whisper, 'Don't worry, I'm sure someone will want you and buy you very soon.'

"As I wandered away, I was quite surprised at what I'd done. Could I be growing fond of the zebra I'd made? It was not really fondness, I decided. I was just feeling a little sorry for it.

"People began to come into the Hall just then, and soon it became filled with voices, and the smell of coats, and the rustle of best dresses. Hats blossomed like flowers against the brown walls, rings shone in the light, children pulled at skirts, hands touched and picked up, and put down, eyes looked, purses came out of bags, and precious bargains were laid in baskets.

"I stood for a long time near the Dolls' Stall, trying to decide whether I wanted another. Dolls are strange: you either take to them or you don't. These dolls all had pouting mouths, hair that was too yellow, gowns that were too fine. I could not imagine loving a single one of them. I moved on.

"Then I saw it. It was a musical

box, playing 'Goodbye, Dolly Gray'. It was the most enchanting thing I had ever seen, and I wanted it with all my heart. The wooden lid was painted in a pattern of plump, pink flowers and glossy blue ribbons, and right in the middle there was a picture of a lady dancing in a shower of tiny, black notes of music: crotchets, and quavers and semi-quavers. The lady's dress was blue, with a full skirt. As soon as I could make myself heard above the noise, I asked the lady behind the stall how much the musical box cost.

" 'What box, dear? Oh, that old thing. That's only a shilling.'

"My fingers crushed the sixpence in my pocket. Only half enough. What was I going to do? My mother would have to give me a whole new sixpence. Maybe she wouldn't want to? I pushed that thought away quickly. Surely she would want me to have the lovely box? Would someone else buy it in the time it would take me to walk to the Soft Toy Stall, and back? They were almost bound to, because it was the prettiest thing in the Hall. I decided to stay near the box all afternoon, and touch it whenever anyone came near it. Then they would think I was buying it. As soon as people began to leave the Hall at the end of the afternoon, I would rush back to my mother and ask for the money.

"The time passed quickly. I played 'Goodbye, Dolly Gray' over and over again, and hardly noticed the other people. After a while, they began to leave the Hall. Outside it was dark. This, I thought, would be a safe moment to rush to my mother and ask her for another sixpence.

"She was sitting on a chair behind her stall, looking very happy. Her hair was a little untidy, and her cheeks were pink.

" 'Mother,' I said, 'I'm so sorry, but I've found just what I'd like and it costs a shilling. Please, *please* can you give me another sixpence?'

" 'Aren't you even going to tell me what it is?' My mother smiled at me.

" 'A musical box, with a dancing lady, and flowers. It plays "Goodbye, Dolly Gray". It's beautiful.'

" 'Well, it sounds very nice, dear, I'm sure.' She pushed some strands of hair away from her forehead. 'As I've done so well and sold nearly all my animals, and since it's nearly Christmas, I suppose you may have an extra sixpence, just this once.'

"I ran behind the stall, and hugged my mother's knees, while she counted out the money. I looked up. My mother had put six separate pennies out on the red cloth of the stall. I noticed, briefly, that my zebra was the only animal that had not been sold, and I felt a little sad for him, but I was longing to go back to my box, and so happy at the thought of owning it, and stroking it, and hearing the twinkling music in my very own room that I forgot about the zebra as soon as I had collected the six pennies together.

"I fled back to pay for my musical box. It was gone. I looked under

the cloth that covered the stall,
under embroidered tray cloths,
behind all the ornaments lying on
the stall. It had gone. I couldn't
believe it. I said to the lady,
'Please, where is the musical
box?'

" 'Sold, dear, I'm afraid,' she
answered, putting things away
into brown boxes. 'Just a few
moments ago. I didn't know you
were interested in buying it.'

"Again, I could not believe it.
Had she not even seen me there,
all afternoon, stroking the lid?
Had she not heard the music?
I stared at the lady's drooping
cheeks, and her plum-coloured

dress and nearly burst with pure anger. I hated her.

"I walked back to my mother's stall. I didn't know where I was. I forgot about people, and bumped into knees and baskets feeling nothing, feeling numbed. All I knew and all I could think of was the deep, black hole of disappointment and loss that had taken the place of all the pleasure I had felt when I thought I owned the box. Gradually, I began to notice what was around me. I was standing beside my mother's stall, and the zebra was looking up at me, quite kindly, I thought. My misery and the zebra's loneliness

63

on the counter became mixed up together. It seemed that no one else wanted him, so he would be mine, after all. I paid my mother a shilling for him. I didn't need the money for anything now, and I thought it would make the zebra feel more important if he were a bought animal, and not simply a leftover. I pulled him off the stall and hugged him. He was soft and comforting. Then I went and sat on the steps by the side of the stage, out of sight of my mother, and wept and wept into the zebra's black-and-white back.

"I don't know how long I sat there, crying, but after a while,

I noticed a shiny pair of black boots on the floor, buttoned firmly around two short legs. Then came a cherry-red skirt, trimmed with white fur, a tight red jacket, with fur at the neck and wrists, and then a face. The face belonged to a girl, with round cheeks and a straight fringe of dark hair. Her eyes were brown and bright and very wide open. She was chewing her bottom lip, and clutching a white fur muff. The string dangled and dragged on the dirty floor.

She said, 'You've been crying for ages.'

" 'Yes,' I managed to mutter.

" 'Have you finished crying now?'

" 'I think so, thank you. I'll cry
again later.'

" 'Why are you crying, anyway?
I wouldn't cry, not with a zebra
like that.'

" 'Do you like it?'

" 'Yes,' said the girl firmly. 'I like
animals. I like sick animals best,

because then I can play animal
hospitals, which is my favourite
game. Your zebra looks *very* sick.
That's why I like him.'

" 'I made him,' I said.

" 'Oh, my!' (the brown eyes
opened wider) 'how clever of you,
to make a sick zebra.'

" 'You can have him. I don't
really want him. I only took him
because I felt sorry for him.
Nobody bought him, you see.'

" 'I would've, if I'd seen him,' said
the girl. 'Thank you, though, very
much, for giving him to me. My
name is Helen Arthur. What's your
name?'

" 'Pinny,' I said. 'Well, Penelope

Sophia Pintle, really, but that's long, so I'm called Pinny.'

" 'I haven't very much I can give you in return, I'm afraid. Only a silly little box thing my nanny bought for me.' From her muff she took out my box, with the dancing lady on it, and almost threw it into my lap.

"I think Helen was very surprised when I jumped up and hugged her. I was quite surprised myself. I even shouted, 'Oh, I love you, Helen, I love you. You're my friend! You are my friend, aren't you?'

" 'I don't really know you, but you look nice. I will be your friend if you like.'

"We held hands and went over to where my mother was putting her coat on.

" 'Is that your mother?' asked Helen.

" 'Yes, in the brown dress.'

" 'She's talking to my nanny.'

" 'Haven't you got a mother?' I wanted to know.

" 'Yes, but she goes out a lot, so Nanny looks after me most of the time.'

"I went up to my mother, and told her about Helen giving me the musical box. Helen said to her nanny, 'Please can Pinny come to tea tomorrow?' And, of course,

Nanny said, 'yes' and my mother said 'yes'."

Aunt Pinny got up.

"Is that the end of the story?" I murmured.

"Yes, and the beginning of my friendship with Helen. We've been friends ever since. She's an elderly lady now, like me, I suppose. But she looks just the same to me as she did then, so many years ago. She still wears a cherry-red coat."

"But how did you come to have the patch for your quilt, if Helen had the zebra?"

Aunt Pinny laughed. "Zebra was operated on in Helen's animal hospital almost immediately. We cut a big piece out of his side and replaced it with a bit of red felt. That was the scar, you see. I kept the cut-out black-and-white piece and sewed it into the quilt. Goodnight, now."

Aunt Pinny switched off the light and went out of the room.

Betsey and the Mighty Marble

Malorie Blackman

"I've got a marble. A mighty marble," said Josh proudly. School had finished for the day and there was still plenty of afternoon left to play in. Betsey and her friends were on the beach.

"Who wants to look at my mighty marble?" Josh called out.

"Me! Me!" everyone shouted.

Josh held out his marble in the palm of his hand. Betsey's brown eyes sparkled brighter than sunshine on the clear blue sea behind her. Ooooh! All eyes were on Josh's marble. Oh, how it glittered! Oh, how it glistened! Betsey had never seen anything like it.

"I told you," said Josh. "Isn't it terrific?"

It was the biggest marble Betsey had ever seen and it was filled with sky blue and leaf green and moonlight silver slivers.

"It's the most beautiful marble in the world," Betsey breathed. And all at once, she wanted that

73

marble. She wanted that marble something fierce.

"Josh," began Betsey, holding up her bag of marbles. "I'll swap you ten of my best marbles for your mighty marble."

"No way," Josh scoffed. "Mr Mighty Marble is staying with me!"

"I'll swap you *twenty* of my marbles for your mighty marble," said May.

Soon the air was filled with "I'll swap you this", and "I'll swap you that", but Josh only laughed and held Mr Mighty Marble up higher.

Betsey looked at the super marble in Josh's hand. It seemed

to be calling out to her, teasing her.

"Betsey . . ." whispered Mr Mighty Marble. "Betsey, look at me. Aren't I just the most perfect, the most splendid marble in the world!" And what could Betsey reply but, "You are! You are!"

Betsey dug her hand into her dress pocket and slowly took out Old Faithful. Old Faithful was a small marble, perfect and clear, with a single gold streak like a summer lightning flash caught in its middle. Betsey's dad had given it to her.

"You look after Old Faithful," said Dad. "And Old Faithful will look after you."

It was Betsey's special marble and all her friends admired it, but Betsey never played with it. Old Faithful was too small to play with.

"Josh," said Betsey. "Let's have a contest, right now. Your Mr Mighty Marble against my best marble."

"Why should I?" frowned Josh.

"'Cause if you win, I'll give you every marble I've got," said Betsey slowly. She held up her full bag of marbles. "You'll get every single marble in here."

Josh's eyes gleamed. "Including Old Faithful?"

Betsey looked at the marble her dad had given her. Next to Mr Mighty Marble, Old Faithful looked dull and titchy-tiny and hardly worth bothering with at all.

"Including Old Faithful," Betsey agreed at last.

"Betsey! You can't do that," said May. "Your dad gave you Old Faithful."

"May, don't you worry," said Betsey. "If I win, I'll get Josh's super marble."

"And what happens if you lose?" asked May, her hands on her hips.

Betsey thought about it, long and hard. If she lost then Josh would end up with every single

marble she had in the world –
including Old Faithful. Dad had
played marbles with Old Faithful
when he was a boy and he'd given
her Old Faithful as a present. How
could she give away a present from
her dad? She shouldn't have told
Josh she'd give him Old Faithful.
What if she *did* lose and Dad
found out?

"Josh, I think . . ." Betsey began.

"You're not changing your mind,
are you? You're not turning
chicken?" Josh called out. "Cluck!
Clu-uu-ck! Chicken!"

"No, I'm not. I'm ready when you
are," said Betsey. But as she spoke
she was careful not to look at May.

That didn't mean that she couldn't hear May tutting beside her, though.

Josh walked to his starting position which was at the end of the path that led to the beach. Everyone followed him. May pulled Betsey back from the crowd.

"Betsey, you're making a big mistake." May shook her head.

"Botheration, May! You're not my gran'ma. Don't you try to boss my head," said Betsey, annoyed.

"Are you really going to let Josh take all your marbles?" asked May. "Even the one your dad gave you?"

"I'm going to win Josh's mighty marble," Betsey said stubbornly. "So Josh won't get any of my marbles. I won't lose a single one of them."

"You've lost your marbles already if you think your itsy-bitsy bit of glass stands a chance against Josh's mighty marble," said May.

Betsey began to feel bad. Worse than bad. Betsey began to feel terrible. She wished she'd never challenged Josh to this stupid contest.

"Come on then, Betsey," Josh called out. "I'm busting to win a whole bag of marbles."

80

Betsey and May walked over to join Josh and the others.

"Josh, we can still have our contest but I don't want to include Old Faithful in it. My dad gave me Old Faithful and—"

But Josh didn't let Betsey finish.

"Cluck! Clu-uu-ck! Chicken!" Josh began to leap about and to peck and flap and strut, just like a chicken. "Cluck! Clu-uu-ck!" Soon everyone else was doing the same thing. "Clu-uu-ck!"

"Botheration!" said Betsey. "Josh, you're about to lose Mr Mighty Marble."

Betsey dug into her bag.

"What are you doing?" Josh frowned.

"Getting out a marble to play with," answered Betsey.

"You've got to use Old Faithful," Josh said. "That was the deal."

"But that's not fair. Your mighty marble is ginormous and Old Faithful is tiddly," said Betsey.

"Too bad. That's the deal," smiled Josh.

What could Betsey do? The contest was all her idea so she couldn't back out now. There was nothing left to do but to stay put and play. Betsey felt her eyes stinging but she forced herself not to cry. She was going to lose all

83

her precious marbles. All the marbles it had taken her so long to collect. And worse still, she was going to lose Old Faithful.

"Josh, you go first," sniffed Betsey.

And the contest began. Everyone gathered round to watch. Josh flicked Mr Mighty Marble first. Betsey flicked Old Faithful away from Mr Mighty Marble. Josh flicked his marble towards Betsey's.

"Ooooh!" A gasp came from everyone around. Josh had only just missed Betsey's marble.

This was it. If Betsey didn't do something, Josh would hit her marble with his very next shot and then Betsey would lose every single marble she had in the world.

"Bombsies!" Betsey said.

Josh laughed. "Bombsies! With that little marble! You can't win, Betsey, so give up now."

"I'll show you," Betsey said. She stood up, Old Faithful in her hand. She stood over Josh's marble carefully lining up Old Faithful over Mr Mighty Marble. If she missed, Josh would win for sure. No one spoke, the only sound came from the waves lapping on the white sand and the sound of birds singing from the trees.

"Your hand can't be lower than

your waist," Josh said.

"I know." Betsey didn't look up. She carried on lining up her shot until Old Faithful was directly above Mr Mighty Marble. Then Betsey let go of her own marble. Old Faithful hit Mr Mighty Marble with a CRR-AAA-CK!

Then a strange thing happened. Old Faithful bounced off Mr Mighty Marble.

"Ooooh!" said everyone.

Josh's marble wasn't well. It wasn't well at all. Mr Mighty Marble, Mr Super Marble, Mr Bigger-than-anyone-else's Marble had cracked into four pieces. Each piece lay on the path, glistening and glittering just as loudly as before.

Betsey picked up Old Faithful and stared at it.

"Wow, Betsey. That's some marble," everyone said.

Josh carefully picked up the pieces that made up what used to be Mr Mighty Marble.

"Look what you did." Josh stared down at the pieces in his hand.

"Mr Mighty Marble doesn't look so mighty any more," May laughed.

"Sorry, Josh," Betsey said. "You can have any five of my marbles if you want." Betsey held out her bag of marbles.

"Can I have Old Faithful?" Josh

asked hopefully.

"No chance!" said Betsey firmly. "Old Faithful may be small, but he's a real super marble."

Josh looked down and kicked at the ground with the toe of his right shoe.

"Come on, Josh," smiled Betsey. "I'll give you my second best marble instead."

"Oh, all right then," Josh said at last. Betsey handed over her bag and let Josh pick out five marbles he wanted.

Then Betsey, May and all their friends set off for home, telling tales of Old Faithful, the mightiest marble of them all.

Tale of a One-Way Street

Joan Aiken

There was a little town which had a one-way street in it. In this town also, the postman carried a walkie-talkie radio set, so that as he went along the streets, putting people's letters through their front doors, he could report all the news back to the post office.

"Mrs Jones got a postcard from her son in Rome. And she's having fried eggs for breakfast."

"Mr Smith's parcel of fish-hooks has come at last. But one of his front windows is broken; it looked as if a bird had flown through it."

"Miss Brown's mother in Ipswich sent her a currant cake. Very good; she just gave me a piece. And her white cat has had kittens in front of the kitchen fire: two, at present."

The people in the post office, who had to spend all day sorting letters into little heaps, one heap for each street, were very pleased to get all this interesting news while they did their dull job.

One morning the postman said,

"I'm at the top of the one-way street. There's a mover's van halfway down the hill. I reckon a new family is moving into the empty house. I'll tell you more later."

And he started down the one-way street, putting letters through people's letter-boxes as he went along.

The name of this street was really Narrow Hill. Because it was so narrow, and so steep, the traffic was only allowed to go down it, never up, and so everyone in the town had fallen into the habit of calling it the one-way street, instead of using its proper name.

"Good morning," said the postman to the new family who were moving their furniture out of the van. "Any letters for you, I wonder?"

"Mann, the name is," said the father. "Mr and Mrs Mann. And young Tom Mann."

"Number Fifty, Mr and Mrs Mann," said the postman writing it down.

"No letters today, but perhaps there'll be some tomorrow."

Mr Mann stuck up a sign that said, T. MANN, PLUMBER. Mrs Mann carried in a last load of sheets and towels. Then the mover's van drove off.

When young Tom Mann put his head out of the front door, after helping to carry in all the furniture, a thrush flying past overhead called,

"Hello, young Tom Mann! You must turn right!"

And a horse trotting past, pulling a cart full of beer barrels, called,

"Turn right, Tom Mann, turn right, clippety-clop, turn right."

"Why must I turn right?" said Tom. "If I turn right, that takes me down to the bottom of the hill. But I want to go up to the top."

"You must turn right because it is a one-way street," said the

postman, walking on down the
hill, putting letters into people's
boxes.

"Good morning, I'm the postman
with one-way feet,
And I walk one way along the
one-way street."
The thrush, flying overhead,
called,
"I'm the bird that nests in your
garden and sings,
And I fly along the one-way street
on one-way wings."
A boy riding past on his bike
shouted,
"I'm Bill, with a bike with a brake
that squeals,
I bike along the one-way street on

one-way wheels."
A girl skated down the road on
roller-skates, calling as she went,
"I'm Susan, a girl who never
stands and waits,
I skate along the one-way street on
one-way skates."
A coal-man with a lorry
delivering coal called down from
his driver's cab,
"I'm the coal-man who carries
the coal for your fires,
I drive along the one-way street on
one-way tyres."
A cat, hurrying along the garden
wall, stopped to say,
"I catch nice mice in my clever
claws,

And I trot along the one-way street
on one-way paws."

A gull called down from high up,
"I float one-way over all the roofs,"
and the horse, pulling his beer
cart, neighed,

"I canter one way on my one-way
hoofs."

And the sun, high overhead in
the sky, winked its great golden
eye as a cloud sailed past
underneath, and said,

"I'm the sun who shines in the
sky so bright,
I travel one way from morning to
night."

"But what happens if I want to
go the other way?" said Tom.

"You'd get run over and squashed flat," said the postman.

"All the birds would bump into you," said the thrush.

"You'd get lost and never come home again," said Bill and Susan.

"Nobody ever *has* gone the other way," said the coal-man. "It's not allowed."

"I don't see why," said Tom, but at that moment his mother put her head out of the front door and said, "Tom, it's time for dinner, and don't let me hear any talk about your going the wrong way along the one-way street. Why, goodness knows where you'd end up! At the North Pole, most likely!"

So Tom went in to dinner, and all the other people went their way down the hill, skating or walking or driving or biking or flying or trotting.

But Tom kept thinking about the one-way street as he ate his boiled egg. Boiled eggs and bread-and-butter was what they had for lunch, because of having just moved into the house. Mrs Mann had not had time to get to the shops yet.

"Mother," said Tom, "how do you boil an egg?"

"There's only one way to boil an egg properly," said his mother.

"You put it into boiling water

and wait till it's done.

> You could keep on boiling
> eggs all day,
> But still there's only one
> right way."

"And how do you make bread and butter?" said Tom.

"There's only one way. You put the butter on the bread and spread it.

> Take loaf, take butter, and
> cut, and spread,
> There's only one way to put
> butter on bread."

"How do you mend a burst pipe?" Tom asked his father.

"There's nobbut one way to do it properly," said Tom's father, and he told Tom how it was done.

"Smooth and solder and work
and wipe,
There's only one way to mend
a pipe."

Tom listened to his father and
his mother, and he said to himself,

"I can see there's only one way to
boil an egg and spread butter and
mend a pipe, but there are *two*
ways to walk along a street, and I
don't see why I'm not allowed to
use them both."

But he didn't say this out loud.
His mother was busy moving
tables and chairs around, to see
which way looked best, and his
father was hard at work, deciding

which things ought to go into which rooms.

Tom went and looked out through the front window at the one-way street. Every moving thing that he could see was going *down* the hill – cars and carts, prams and bikes, ladies and dogs and pushchairs and bakers' vans.

"Just the same," thought Tom, "some day I am going *up* that hill, to find out where it goes."

Next day Tom went down the hill to school at the bottom. And there he learned to read.

"There's only one way to learn reading," said the teacher. "You

have to start with letters.

There's just one way and that is
that C-A-T spells nothing but cat."
Next Tom learned sums.
"There's only one way, there aren't
any more
Two plus two makes only four."
On his way home from school
Tom thought harder than ever
about the one-way street. He had
to go home a different way, which
took longer, along Traders' Lane,
and Market Hill, and Church
Walk, and Parson's Steps, which
brought him out at the top of
Narrow Hill, and then he could
run down the street to his home.

Each day at school the lessons

were just the same, until they came
to Friday. On Friday they had
painting, and the painting teacher
was somebody new, somebody Tom
had not seen before.

When Tom asked,

"What is the proper way to paint
a picture?" this teacher said,

"There isn't any right way. There
are hundreds of ways, and each
one is different. You just have to
take your courage in your hands
and begin."

Tom didn't know how to take his
courage in his hands, but he took
paper and brushes and paints, and
he painted a picture of Narrow
Hill, the one-way street, with the

houses going right up the hill and off the top of the paper.

Susan looked over her shoulder and said, "You silly boy! There ought to be *sky* at the top, not houses. And who ever heard of a *pink cat*?"

Bill looked over his shoulder and said, "All the things in your picture are going the wrong way, if that is meant to be our street. And I never yet saw a dark-blue horse. You must be crazy!"

But the teacher looked at Tom's picture and said, "You keep on exploring that avenue, boy, and you may find out a secret or two, by and by."

Tom was surprised, because he thought his picture was of a street, not an avenue, but he was pleased when the teacher put it up on the wall and stuck a gold star on it.

Next morning was Saturday, so there was no school. It was a quiet, foggy, misty, grey, empty day which seemed to have no beginning or middle or end. The sun didn't even try to shine through the fog. Tom's mother was painting the bathroom walls, and his father was fixing the kitchen taps, both very busy, so Tom thought, "Now is my chance."

He put on his long woolly scarf,

and he took his courage in both
hands, now that he knew how, and
he went out of the front door and
turned left up the hill, into the
thick, white, woolly fog. It was
very queer, rather like being inside
a white parcel, and at first Tom
didn't much care for it.

But then he heard a pit-a-pat
noise, and he saw a bright pink cat
trotting along just ahead of him.

"Hello, young Tom Mann," said
the cat. "Going my way?"

"Yes, I think so, thank you," said
Tom, and he followed the pink
cat.

Now beyond the pink cat he
noticed a yellow seagull and a

silver thrush, flying through the mist.

"Hello, Tom," they called. "Are you going our way?"

"Yes, I believe so, thank you," said Tom.

Next he saw a pea-green postman with a sack of mail, and a bright red coal-man, whose lorry was stacked with scarlet bags of coal.

"Good morning, Tom," they said. "Going our way, are you?"

"Yes, thank you," said Tom. And then he saw a dark-blue horse, and a golden girl on roller-skates, and an orange boy on a bike.

"Hi there, Tom," they called.

"Are you going our way?"

"Yes I am," said Tom.

Then he came to the top of the hill. There was the sun, standing still overhead and shining bright violet rays down across the country on the other side of the hill. The fog stopped here like a wall. Tom, and all the people with him, could see for miles and miles into the land that lay beyond, but they could not see right across, because the country was far too wide.

What they could see was very surprising.

They saw a whole mountain of boiled eggs, each one different from all the others. They saw a whole field paved with slices of bread-and-butter, no two of them alike. They saw a great forest of pipes, each pipe mended in a different way. They saw streams and fountains of letters and numbers sparkling in the purple rays of the sun, making hundreds and thousands of different words, giving the answers to any number of sums. And all the words were right, and all were different. All the sums were right and all were different.

In the middle, on a sunny hillside, under a tree covered in cherries the size of apples, or

apples the colour of cherries, was
a comfortable chair with a label on
it that said TOM.

"Now I know," said Tom to the
cat and the gull and the thrush
and the postman and the coal-man
and the horse and the boy and the
girl, "that while I thought I was
coming your way, *you* were coming
my way. And now I know about
this place, I shall come here as
often as I like."

He sat down comfortably in the
chair and watched three lemon-
yellow fish jumping in the
fountain, catching the numbers in
their mouths.

The cat chased a pink mouse, the

postman delivered half a dozen pea-green letters, and the dark-blue horse nibbled a clump of red primroses.

When Tom went home, he found his mother still painting the bathroom and his father still fixing the kitchen taps. Neither of them had noticed that he had been gone.

"Oh, Tom," said his mother. "Run down the hill, will you, and buy me a bottle of Jollyclens, that's the only stuff to get paint off paintbrushes."

"And while you're at it," said his father, "get me a packet of Smith's

Superfine Staples. Don't get any other kind."

"OK," said Tom, and he took the money his mother gave him and went out of the front door, turning right and running down the steep hill, going the same way as all the cars and horses and prams and bikes and vans and ladies with their dogs. For now the fog had lifted and he could see everything as plain as plain.

He bought the Jollyclens and the Smith's Superfine Staples, and went back, taking the way he came after school, by Traders' Lane, and Market Hill, and Church Walk, and Parsons' Steps, and so to the top of Narrow Hill, from where he could run all the way to his front door. And as he ran he sang,

"I'm Tom, the boy with one-way feet
And I run one way along the one-way street."

When he got home he gave his mother the bottle of Jollyclens and he said to her, "Mum."

"Well?"

"You *can't* walk more than one way at a time, can you?"

"Of course you can't," said his mother. "Don't be silly. And go and put on the kettle for tea. I've made a very nice new kind of cake. It's on the shelf in the larder."

The postman, on his walkie-talkie set, reported back to the post office, "The new family, halfway up Narrow Hill, seems to be settling in nicely."

How the Whale Got His Throat

Rudyard Kipling

In the sea, once upon a time, O my Best Beloved, there was a Whale, and he ate fishes. He ate the starfish and the garfish, and the crab and the dab, and the plaice and the dace, and the skate and his mate, and the mackerel and the pickereel, and the really truly twirly-whirly eel. All the fishes he could find in all the sea he ate with his mouth – so! Till at last there was only one small fish left in all the sea, and he was a small 'Stute Fish, and he swam a little behind the Whale's right ear, so as to be out of harm's way. Then the Whale stood up on his tail and said, "I'm hungry." And the small 'Stute Fish said in a small 'stute voice, "Noble and generous Cetacean, have you ever tasted Man?"

"No," said the Whale. "What is it like?"

"Nice," said the small 'Stute Fish. "Nice but nubbly."

"Then fetch me some," said the

Whale, and he made the sea froth up with his tail.

"One at a time is enough," said the 'Stute Fish. "If you swim to latitude Fifty North, longitude Forty West (that is Magic), you will find, sitting *on* a raft, *in* the middle of the sea, with nothing on but a pair of blue canvas breeches, a pair of suspenders (you must *not* forget the suspenders, Best Beloved), and a jack-knife, one shipwrecked Mariner, who, it is only fair to tell you, is a man of infinite-resource-and-sagacity."

So the Whale swam and swam to latitude Fifty North, longitude Forty West, as fast as he could swim, and *on* a raft, *in* the middle of the sea, *with* nothing to wear except a pair of blue canvas breeches, a pair of suspenders (you must particularly remember the suspenders, Best Beloved), *and* a jack-knife, he found one single, solitary shipwrecked Mariner, trailing his toes in the water. (He had his mummy's leave to paddle, or else he would never have done it, because he was a man of infinite-resource-and-sagacity.)

Then the Whale opened his mouth back and back and back till it nearly touched his tail, and he swallowed the shipwrecked Mariner, and the raft he was

119

sitting on, and his blue canvas breeches, and the suspenders (which you *must* not forget), *and* the jack-knife. He swallowed them all down into his warm, dark, inside cupboards, and then he smacked his lips – so, and turned round three times on his tail.

But as soon as the Mariner, who was a man of infinite-resource-and-sagacity, found himself truly inside the Whale's warm, dark, inside cupboards, he stumped and he jumped and he thumped and he bumped, and he pranced and he danced, and he banged and he clanged, and he hit and he bit, and he leaped and he creeped, and he prowled and he howled, and he hopped and he dropped, and he cried and he sighed, and he crawled and he bawled, and he stepped and he lepped, and he danced hornpipes where he shouldn't, and the Whale felt most unhappy indeed. (*Have* you forgotten the suspenders?)

So he said to the 'Stute Fish, "This man is very nubbly, and besides he is making me hiccough. What shall I do?"

"Tell him to come out," said the 'Stute Fish.

So the Whale called down his own throat to the shipwrecked Mariner, "Come out and behave yourself. I've got the hiccoughs."

"Nay, nay!" said the Mariner. "Not so, but far otherwise. Take me to my natal-shore and the white-cliffs-of-Albion, and I'll think about it." And he began to dance more than ever.

"You had better take him home,"

said the 'Stute Fish to the Whale. "I ought to have warned you that he is a man of infinite-resource-and-sagacity."

So the Whale swam and swam and swam, with both flippers and his tail, as hard as he could for the hiccoughs; and at last he saw the Mariner's natal-shore and the white-cliffs-of-Albion, and he rushed halfway up the beach, and opened his mouth wide and wide and wide, and said, "Change here for Winchester, Ashuelot, Nashua, Keene, and stations on the *Fitch*burg Road"; and just as he said "Fitch" the Mariner walked out of his mouth. But while the

Whale had been swimming, the Mariner, who was indeed a person of infinite-resource-and-sagacity, had taken his jack-knife and cut up the raft into a little square grating all running criss-cross, and he had tied it firm with his suspenders (*now* you know why you were not to forget the suspenders!), and he dragged that grating good and tight into the Whale's throat, and there it stuck! Then he recited the following *Sloka*, which, as you have not heard it, I will proceed to relate:

*"By means of a grating
I have stopped your ating."*

For the mariner he was also an Hi-ber-ni-an. And he stepped out on the shingle, and went home to his mother, who had given him leave to trail his toes in the water; and he married and lived happily every afterward. So did the Whale. But from that day on, the grating in his throat, which he could neither cough up nor swallow down, prevented him from eating anything except very, very small fish: and that is the reason why whales nowadays never eat men or boys or little girls.

The small 'Stute Fish went and hid himself in the mud under the Door-sills of the Equator. He was afraid that the Whale might be angry with him.

The Sailor took the jack-knife home. He was wearing the blue canvas breeches when he walked out on the shingle. The suspenders were left behind, you see, to tie the grating with: and that is the end of *that* tale.

When the cabin port-holes are
   dark and green
     Because of the seas outside;
When the ship goes *wop* (with a
   wiggle between)
     And the steward falls into the
   soup-tureen,
And the trunks begin to slide:

When the Nursery lies on the floor
   in a heap.
And Mummy tells you to let her
   sleep,
And you aren't waked or washed
   or dressed,
Why, then you will know (if you
   haven't guessed)
You're "Fifty North and Forty
   West!"

Hair of a Cat

Pat Thomson

At two o'clock in the morning the family were awakened by the most appalling screech. Ben, his heart racing, jumped out of bed and ran straight to his parents' room. He could hear Hannah crying and his mother was already hurrying across the landing to snatch her out of her cot. His father was also on his feet, standing at the top of the stairs.

Ben saw him pause, look around for a weapon and seize the only available item. It was a large teddy bear. He grasped it purposefully by the leg. Ben knew it had a very hard head but he also knew the leg came off.

The noise was coming from the kitchen and was accompanied by the sound of breaking china and furniture falling. The family stood on the stairs, Dad carrying the bear, Ben behind him, holding up his pyjama trousers and Mum bringing up the rear, with Hannah in her arms. Ben knew what Dad had to do now. He had to burst through the kitchen door, yelling

"Freeze!" but it didn't seem the same with a bear.

Dad made up his mind. He stepped forward, opened the kitchen door – and groaned.

Peering round Dad's elbow, Ben looked into the room. Minette, their little black cat, was standing rigid on the draining board. Her tail was straight out and her fur reminded Ben of his experiments with iron filings. Broken crockery littered the floor, a chair had been overturned and tomorrow's cornflakes spilled from the box all over the table. Crouched by Minette's food bowl was the cause of all the trouble. Ben stared straight into the unwinking marmalade eyes of the biggest ginger tom he had ever seen.

"I told you that cat flap was a mistake," said Mum.

Minette took several days to get over it. She said as much to Roddy, the dog who lived next door.

"A monster! A great ginger monster! And it's been back."

Roddy sighed. "You don't know how to look after yourself, girl," he said gruffly. "You gotta face up to these bullies."

"But it's enormous," squeaked Minette. "I get in the cupboard and keep quiet. I always leave a bit in my food bowl, though. I'd be afraid not to."

"Well, here's where I've got good news for you. My lot are having a weekend in Derbyshire and they want your lot to look after me."

"You mean you'll be staying the weekend? That would be a shock for the great beast."

"Exactly," said Roddy, smugly.

On Friday afternoon, Roddy's basket was brought round, his lead was hung behind the back door and several tins of dog food were stacked in the kitchen cupboard.

Minette had known Roddy since she was a kitten and felt safe with him. Not that he was a big dog. He was rather small. Postmen, however, treated him with respect and the milkman came early. The neighbour on the other side had called him "a vicious little runt", but at the time there had been a coolness between him and Roddy's owner. She had bought a large mower and had been through his fence and halfway across his rhubarb before she found the "off" switch.

Now, Roddy stalked the kitchen, sniffing experimentally and inspecting the cat flap.

"It's been here, all right," he said. "Pooh! Very nasty! We'll smell it coming. Now, let's place the troops. Minette, you get up on the draining board, and I'll station myself by the cat flap. Stay clear, unless, of course, you want to come down and nip it on the leg when I've got it down. Feel free."

Roddy settled himself. He waited a long time. He had a good

scratch, got up and stretched his legs and settled down again. He began to think of his basket. He wondered what Derbyshire was like. He wondered whether eight tins of dog food were enough for a weekend. What if they didn't come back for a week? Could he last on seven tins? Six tins? Five? Four? Three . . .

When Roddy jerked into wakefulness, it was because his nose was full of a ferocious odour of cat. It was so strong he felt faint. He opened his eyes on a ginger landscape. The cat was so near it blocked his view of the kitchen. It was looking at him.

Roddy was mesmerised by the marmalade eyes. He struggled to his feet. The cat and he were the same size. His hair rose on his shoulders and he growled.

The cat simply growled back, and it was the most controlled, menacing growl Roddy had ever heard. He watched the cat's fur rising until the creature seemed twice as big. It was turning into a lion as he stared at it.

Then, without making any further noise, the cat silently raked Roddy's face with its claws, turned, and slid out of the cat flap.

Minette was very upset. She was

angry with herself for sleeping, horrified by Roddy's scratches and puzzled by what had happened. There was no sign of a struggle and Roddy was very quiet. They retreated to the warm patch behind the garden shed and started all over again.

"We've got to get it tonight," said Roddy. "After that, you're on your own again."

"But what can we do?" wailed Minette.

"No defeatist talk," said Roddy, sharply. "It's a monster, and that's the truth, but when you get a big bully, my girl, forget the muscle. Start using your brains."

137

By the evening, they had made a hundred plans, all useless. They ate their dinners in silence and both left a little food in their bowls.

"I'm still thinking," Minette assured Roddy, "but I'll do it from the draining board." She leaped up, dislodging the washing-up mop which Ben had left in a bowl of water. Roddy happened to be standing right underneath.

"Thank *you*," he snapped. "My brain's all wet now. How can I think with a wet brain?"

"Sorry, Roddy."

"No! Wait! That's it! Get down here, Minette. Help me with our water bowls. If I can get just one go at that ginger mug, I'll be satisfied . . ."

Ben was disturbed by a regular knocking noise. *Flap*! Pause, *flap*! It was in the kitchen again. He padded downstairs and opened the door, quietly. Roddy was sitting by the back door with a washing-up mop in his mouth. As Ben watched, he dipped it into one of the water bowls and waited. The cat flap swung open and the large ginger tom thrust its head in. Roddy smacked it hard with the dripping mop. The flap dropped as the big cat withdrew. It was angry but puzzled, and tried again. This time, Roddy caught it on the nose. It sneezed and jumped back, getting momentarily stuck. While it hissed and spat, Roddy took the opportunity to strike again. His weapon was clumsy but unpleasantly wet and the ginger monster didn't like it. It scrambled backwards in undignified haste and the flap fell. They heard the sound of its claws on the fence as it escaped into the next garden. Ben smiled sleepily and went back to bed.

The next morning, Ben tried to tell his mother what had happened, but the bowls were back in their places and the wet patches had dried. Roddy and Minette were curled up, sleeping late.

"Honestly, Mum! *Wham*! it went, *wham*! on the cat's nose!"

"Really, Ben, Roddy couldn't have worked out something like that. I expect you were dreaming."

She smiled to herself and swept over to the sink. Then, she paused and picked up the mop. Slowly, with finger and thumb, she picked off a long, ginger hair.

Fat Lawrence

Dick King-Smith

Cats come in roughly three
sizes – skinny, middling or
fat. There is a fourth size – very
fat.

But seldom do you see such a one
as Lawrence Higgins. Lawrence
was a cat of a fifth size – very, very
fat indeed. He was black, and so
big and heavy that his owner, Mrs
Higgins of Rosevale, Forest Street,
Morchester, could not lift him even

an inch from the ground.

"Oh, Lawrence Higgins!" she would say (she had named the cat after her late husband, even though he had actually been quite small and thin). "Oh, Lawrence Higgins! Why are you so fat? It isn't as though I overfeed you. You only get one meal a day."

And this was true. At around eight o'clock in the morning Lawrence would come into Rosevale through the cat flap, from wherever he'd been since the previous day, to receive his breakfast.

Then, when he had eaten the big bowl of cat-meat which

Mrs Higgins put before him, he would hoist his black bulk into an armchair and sleep till midday. Then out he would go again, where to Mrs Higgins never knew. She had become used to the fact that her cat only ever spent the mornings at Rosevale.

Five doors further down Forest Street, at Hillview, Mr and Mrs Norman also had a cat, a black cat, the fattest black cat you ever saw.

"Oh, Lawrence Norman!" Mrs Norman would say (they knew his name was Lawrence, they'd read it on a disc attached to his collar, that day, months ago now, when he had suddenly appeared on their window sill, mewing – at lunchtime, it was). "Oh, Lawrence Norman! Why are you so fat?"

"It isn't as though you overfeed him," said Mr Norman.

"No," said his wife. "He only gets one meal a day."

And this was true. At lunchtime Mrs Norman would hear Lawrence mewing and let him in and give him a bowl of cat-meat.

Then, when he had eaten it, he would heave his black bulk on to the sofa and sleep till teatime. Then off he would go again, the Normans never knew where. They'd become accustomed to the

146

fact that their cat only spent the afternoon at Hillview.

Round the corner, in the next street, Woodland Way, there lived at Number 33 an old man called Mr Mason, alone save for his enormously fat black cat. It had slipped in through his back door one day months ago – at teatime it was – and he had read its name on its collar.

"Oh, Lawrence Mason!" he would say as, hearing that scratch on the back door, he let the cat in, and put down a bowl of cat-meat. "Oh, Lawrence Mason! Why are you so fat? It isn't as if I overfeed you. I only give you this one meal a day and that's the truth."

When Lawrence Mason had emptied the bowl, he would stretch his black bulk out on the hearth rug and sleep till suppertime. Then out he would go again, where to old Mr Mason did not know. All he knew was that his cat only spent the evening at Number 33.

In front of Woodland Way was a Park, and on the other side of the Park the houses were larger and posher. In one of them, The Gables, Pevensey Place, lived Colonel and Mrs Barclay-Lloyd and their cat, who had arrived one evening at suppertime, months ago now, wearing a collar with his name on it.

Mrs Barclay-Lloyd had opened the front door of The Gables, and there, sitting at the top of the flight of steps that led up from the street, was this enormously fat black cat.

Each evening now at suppertime the Barclay-Lloyds would set before Lawrence a dish of chicken nuggets and a saucer of Gold Top milk.

"Lawrence Barclay-Lloyd!" the Colonel would say. "I cannot understand why you are so fat."

"To look at him," his wife would say, "anyone would think he was getting four meals a day instead of just the one that we give him."

When Lawrence had eaten his chicken and drunk his milk, he would hump his black bulk up the stairs, and clamber on to the foot of the Barclay-Lloyds' four-poster bed, and fall fast asleep.

The Colonel and his wife took to going to bed early too, knowing that around seven o'clock next morning they would be woken by their cat mewing loudly to be let out of The Gables. They never knew where he went, only that they would not see him again until the following evening.

For a long while Lawrence was not

only the fattest but also the happiest cat you can imagine. Assured of comfortable places to sleep and the certainty of four good square meals a day, he had not a care in the world.

But gradually, as time went on and he grew, would you believe it, even fatter, he began to feel that all this travelling – from Rosevale to Hillview, from Hillview to Number 33, from Number 33 to The Gables, and then back from The Gables all the way to Rosevale – was too much of a good thing. All that walking, now that his black bulk was so vast, was tiring. In addition, he suffered from indigestion.

One summer evening while making his way from Woodland Way to Pevensey Place for supper, he stopped at the edge of a small boating-lake in the middle of the Park.

As he bent his head to lap, he caught sight of his reflection in the water.

"Lawrence, my boy," he said. "You are carrying too much weight. You'd better do something about it. But what? I'll see what the boys say."

The "boys" were Lawrence's four particular friends. Each lived near one of his addresses.

Opposite Rosevale, on the other side of Forest Street, Fernmount was the home of a ginger tom called Bert, who of course knew the black cat as Lawrence Higgins. Next day after breakfast, Lawrence paid a call on him.

"Bert," he said. "D'you think I'm carrying too much weight?"

"If you carry much more, Higgins, old pal," said Bert, "you'll break your blooming back. Mrs Higgins must feed you well."

"She only gives me one meal a day," Lawrence said.

After lunch, he visited the second of the boys, who also lived in Forest Street, at Restholm, a

153

couple of doors beyond Hillview. He was a tabby tom named Fred, who of course knew the black cat as Lawrence Norman.

"Fred," said Lawrence. "Tell me straight, tom to tom. Would you call me fat?"

"Norman, old chum," said Fred. "You are as fat as a pig. The Normans must shovel food into you."

"They only give me one meal a day," said Lawrence.

After tea he waddled round the corner into Woodland Way, where at Number 35 there lived a white tom called Percy. He of course knew the black cat as

Lawrence Mason.

"Percy," said Lawrence. "Give me some advice . . ."

Percy, like many white cats, was rather deaf.

"Give you some of my mice?" he said. "Not likely, Mason, old mate, you don't need any extra food, anyone can see that. You eat too much already."

"Do you think I should go on a diet?" asked Lawrence.

"Do I think you're going to die of it?" said Percy. "Yes, probably. Old Mason must be stuffing food into you."

"He only gives me one meal a day," said Lawrence loudly.

155

Percy heard this.

"One meal a week, Mason," he said. "That's all you need."

Later, Lawrence plodded across the Park (being careful not to look at his reflection in the boating-lake), and in Pevensey Place he called in at The Cedars, which was opposite The Gables. Here lived the fourth of the boys, a Blue Persian tom by the name of Darius.

Darius was not only extremely handsome with his small wide-set ears and his big round eyes and his snub nose and his long flowing blue coat. He was also much more intelligent than Bert or Fred or Percy.

"What's up, Barclay-Lloyd, old
boy?" he said when he saw
Lawrence. "You're puffing and
blowing like a grampus. You're
going to have to do something
about yourself, you know."

"The Colonel and his wife only
feed me once a day," said
Lawrence.

"I dare say," replied Darius. "But look here, Barclay-Lloyd, old boy, I wasn't born yesterday, you know. You're getting more than one meal a day, aren't you now?"

"Yes," said Lawrence.

"How many?"

"Four altogether."

"So at three other houses besides The Gables?"

"Yes."

"Bad show, Barclay-Lloyd," said Darius. "You'll have to cut down. If you don't, then in my opinion you're going to eat yourself to death. Just think how much better you'll feel if you lose some of that weight. You won't get so puffed,

158

you'll be leaner and fitter, and your girlfriend will find you much more attractive."

"I haven't got a girlfriend, Darius," said Lawrence sadly.

"And why is that, Barclay-Lloyd, old boy?" said Darius. "Ask yourself why."

"Because I'm too fat?"

"Undoubtedly."

"A figure of fun, would you say?"

"Afraid so."

"Actually, girls do tend to giggle at me."

"Not surprised."

Lawrence took a deep breath. "All right," he said. "I'll do it,

Darius. I'll go on a diet."

"Good show, Barclay-Lloyd," said Darius.

"I'll cut down to three meals a day," said Lawrence.

"One."

"Two?"

"One," said Darius firmly. "One good meal a day is all any cat needs."

For a little while Lawrence sat, thinking.

Then he said, "But if I'm only to have one meal a day, I only need to go to one house."

"What's wrong with The Gables?" asked Darius.

"Nothing," said Lawrence. "They

give me chicken nuggets and Gold Top milk."

"What!" said Darius. "Well, you can cut the milk out, for a start. Water for you from now on, old boy."

"But if I just stay here," said Lawrence, "the other people will be worried. They'll wonder where I've got to – Mrs Higgins and the Normans and old Mr Mason. And I shan't see the other boys – Bert and Fred and Percy."

For a little while Darius sat, thinking.

Then he said, "There are two ways to play this, Barclay-Lloyd. One is – you continue to make the rounds of your houses, but in each you only eat a quarter of what they put before you. Then that'll add up to one meal a day. Are you strong-minded enough to leave three-quarters of a bowlful at each meal?"

"No," said Lawrence.

"Then," said Darius, "the only thing to do is for you to spend the whole day at each house, in turn. And if you take my advice, you'll cut out breakfast, lunch and tea. Stick to supper. Which reminds me, it's time for mine. Cheerio, Barclay-Lloyd, old boy, and the best of luck with your diet."

To the surprise of the Colonel

and his wife, that Sunday evening
Lawrence didn't touch his milk.
He ate the chicken, certainly,
greedily in fact, as though it was
his last meal for some time, and he
went to sleep on the foot of the
four-poster as usual. But the next
morning no mewing roused the
Barclay-Lloyds, and when they did
wake, it was to find Lawrence still
with them and apparently in no
hurry to move.

On Monday, breakfast time came
and went with no sign of
Lawrence Higgins at Rosevale.

Lunchtime in Hillview passed
without Lawrence Norman.

At Number 33 Lawrence Mason

did not appear for tea.

Old Mr Mason was worried about his black cat, as were the Normans. So was Mrs Higgins, but her worry ceased as Lawrence popped in through the cat flap at Rosevale that evening.

"Lawrence Higgins!" she cried. "Where *have* you been? You must be starving."

Lawrence would have agreed, could he have understood her words, and he polished off the bowl of cat-meat that was put before him and hoisted his black bulk into the armchair and, much to Mrs Higgins' surprise, spent the night there.

On Tuesday evening Lawrence Norman appeared for supper at Hillview.

On Wednesday evening Lawrence Mason ate at Number 33.

Not until the Thursday evening did Lawrence Barclay-Lloyd reappear for supper at The Gables, much to the relief of the Colonel and his wife, who of course had not set eyes on their black cat since Sunday.

Gradually everyone grew used to this strange new state of affairs – that their black cat now only turned up every four days.

And gradually, as the weeks passed, Lawrence grew thinner.

The boys noticed this (although only one of them knew why).

"You on a diet, Higgins, old pal?" asked Bert.

"Sort of," said Lawrence.

"You're looking a lot fitter, Norman, old chum," said Fred.

"I feel it," said Lawrence.

To Percy he said, "I've lost some weight."

"What's that, Mason, old mate?" said Percy.

"I've lost some weight."

"Lost your plate?" said Percy.

"No, weight."

"Eh?"

"*Weight!*" shouted Lawrence.

"Why should I?" said Percy.

"What am I meant to be waiting for?"

As for Darius, he was delighted that his plan for his friend was working so well.

After months of dieting, Lawrence was positively slim.

"Jolly good show, Barclay-Lloyd, old boy," purred the Persian. "The girls will never be able to resist you."

"I don't know any."

"Well, between you and me and the gatepost," said Darius, "there's a little cracker living down at the other end of Pevensey Place. White, she is. Dream of a figure.

Amazing orange eyes. You'd make a grand pair."

So next morning Lawrence woke the Barclay-Lloyds early, left The Gables and made his way down Pevensey Place. I don't expect I shall like her, he thought, Darius was probably exaggerating. But when he caught sight of her, lying in the sunshine on her front lawn, his heart leaped within his so much less bulky body.

"Hello," he said in a voice made gruff by embarrassment.

"Hello," she replied in a voice like honey, and she opened wide her amazing orange eyes.

"I haven't seen you around

168

before," she said. "What's your name?"

"Lawrence," muttered Lawrence.

"I'm Bella," she said.

Bella, thought Lawrence. What a beautiful name! And what a beautiful cat! It's love at first sight! It's now or never!

"Bella," he said. "Could we be . . . friends?"

Bella stood up and stretched her elegant white body.

"Friends, yes, I dare say," she replied. "But nothing more."

"Oh," said Lawrence. "You don't fancy me?"

"Frankly, Lawrence, no," said Bella. "I like the sound of you – you're nice, I'm sure – but you're much too slender for my taste, I've never cared for slim boys. I go for really well-covered types. As a matter of fact there's a black cat further up Pevensey Place – I haven't seen him about lately – but I really had a crush on him. Talk about fat, he was enormous! I do love a very, very fat cat, and

170

he was the fattest!"

She sighed.

"If only I could meet him again one day," she said.

You will! thought Lawrence. You will, and before very long too, and he padded away across the Park to be in time for breakfast at Rosevale, followed by lunch at Hillview, tea at Number 33, and then back for supper at The Gables, including a saucer of Gold Top and perhaps, if he could persuade the Barclay-Lloyds, second helpings. Oh, Bella, he thought as he hurried along. You just wait!

Mr Gill Makes a Wish

Margaret Joy

Mr Gill was busy in his office. He was sitting behind his big desk, thinking about Allotment Lane School and all the jobs that needed to be done.

First of all there was the hole in the roof. Every time it rained, the Big Boys and Girls in the top class had to put buckets and cloths on the floor to catch the drops that dripped down through the ceiling on to the floor of their classroom.

And today the sky looked *very* dark and cloudy. Mr Gill felt sure the rain would soon come pouring down – on to the roof, then in through the ceiling, then drip, drip, drip on to the floor. Oh dear! He sneezed a very loud sneeze.

"And another thing that's bothering me," thought Mr Gill to himself, "is the dinner trays. Some of the children seem to be butterfingers these days. They stand in the line for dinners, chatting to their friends and forgetting that they're holding their plastic tray ready for dinner. Then – C-R-A-S-H! Everyone jumps and looks round – another tray is broken, or at least cracked. Then I have to order more new trays."

Mr Gill sneezed two very loud sneezes, then looked at the pile of letters on his desk.

"Have I got to answer all these?" he groaned. He was talking to himself, and it was a silly question, because he knew he had to, just as he knew that later on he had to talk to Mr Loftus the caretaker about the broken window in the kitchen; someone had kicked a football through it by mistake.

Then he knew he had to phone the school photographer who was coming to take photographs of the children. After that, Mr Loftus was going to show him two broken chairs – so that would mean ordering two new ones. Then one of the children's mothers was coming to see him because her little boy wasn't getting on with his reading, and she wanted to find out why. After that, one of the fathers was coming to see him because he thought there was too much fighting in the playground. Miss Mee was coming to see him to ask for some money to buy new books for the school library; then Mrs Owthwaite's children were going to show him how well they were getting on with their number work. And Mr Gill knew that some children in Class 3 had promised to come and show him the big fat toad they had found on the school field. Later on, when Mrs Hubb, the school secretary, had counted all the dinner money, he would have to drive with it to the bank.

Mr Gill thought it all sounded like a *very* busy morning.

"Oh dear, oh dear!" he said, and sneezed three very loud sneezes, so that his eyes watered and the walls shook. In the next room Mrs Hubb put her hands over her ears.

"And I think I've got a cold coming too," said Mr Gill to

himself. He blew his nose very noisily and looked out of the window: it was pouring with rain.

"Oh no," said poor Mr Gill, "not rain! That's the limit, the absolute limit! Just for today, I wish . . . I wish that everyone in the school would *disappear* and leave me alone!"

He sat for five minutes holding his aching head in his hands. He sighed and sneezed four very loud sneezes, then started to read his pile of letters.

"There," he said, half an hour later and much more cheerful. "I've read all those letters. I'll just go and ask Mrs Hubb if she'll type the answers to them."

He went next door into her tiny office – but she wasn't there. "That's funny," thought Mr Gill. "Never mind, I'll go and see if the rain's come through the ceiling in the top class."

He walked along to the classroom and noticed a damp patch on the ceiling, but there wasn't a pool of water on the floor, so this made him even more cheerful.

"But where are the children?" he suddenly wondered. There was no sign of the children or their teacher. Everything was strangely quiet.

"That's very odd indeed," thought Mr Gill, feeling a little less cheerful after all. "I'd better go and look in all the other classrooms."

He did. He looked into every single room, and every single room was *completely* empty. There wasn't another person to be seen. Everything was absolutely silent.

"Oh my goodness," said Mr Gill. "What was it I said earlier? I wish that everyone in the school would *disappear and leave me alone*. And now they have! My wish has come true. I've lost everyone in the school! Oh dear, oh dear, oh dear!"

179

And he sneezed five extremely loud sneezes.

"What shall I tell Mr Hubb has happened to his wife? What shall I tell the teachers' husbands and wives? How can I tell all the mothers and fathers that their children have disappeared? Oh dear, oh dear!"

Mr Gill's head was aching so much that he thought he'd better go outside for some fresh air. He looked out of the window. The rain had stopped and the sun had come out. He stepped out of the school door and into the playground – and stood still.

There, in the middle of the

playground was Mrs Hubb, *and* all
the children from all the classes,
and all their teachers. Mr Gill
suddenly felt very relieved that he
hadn't made them all disappear
with his silly wish.

"*There* you all are, thank
goodness," he said, but nobody
heard him – they were all looking
up at the sky. Mr Gill shaded his
eyes against the bright sunshine.

"What is it?" he asked.

"A rainbow," said Mrs Hubb.
"Isn't it beautiful? Look – it
stretches right across the sky over
Allotment Lane School. All the
teachers wanted to bring the
children outside to see such a

181

beautiful rainbow, and so I thought I'd come out too."

She looked at Mr Gill and said, "But we didn't disturb you, because we knew you were very busy – I hope you didn't think we'd disappeared, did you?"

"Um . . . er . . . no, no, of course not. Of course not," said Mr Gill quickly. "But I'm glad I've seen the rainbow. It's made me feel quite cheerful again. Even my cold feels a little better."

He smiled at everyone. Then he gave one more sneeze – just a little one this time – and went back to his room.

The Little Goldfish

Geraldine Kaye

When Bo woke up, he
smiled at the bedroom
ceiling because it was Saturday
and he didn't have to go to school.
He had been at school in Hong
Kong a long time ago, but then his
family bought tickets and flew
across miles of blue-green sea and
now Bo went to school in England
and he didn't like it much. He had
been at Oak Road School for a

term and a bit but he still couldn't
speak much English. He knew
"OK" and "thank you" and
"sorry" and "can't" and as he
helped Father in the take-away at
night he knew "very quick food"
and "what number you want?" but
that was just about all.

"Oh, yes, you're the boy from the
take-away on the corner, aren't
you?" Miss Smith had said on his
first day at school. "This is Bo Lee.
Who is going to look after Bo Lee
for me?" she asked.

"I will," said Charlie, putting up
his hand. "I live next door to the
Ho Ho Take-Away." Class Two
giggled a bit and Bo giggled too,

185

though he had no idea what was funny. "Ho Ho, Bo," somebody whispered. "Ho Ho, Bo."

"Well, it's got Ho Ho Take-Away written over the door," Charlie went on explaining. "And then it's empty space and then it's my house so I can look after Bo easy."

"Thank you, Charlie," Miss Smith said. And Charlie did look after Bo. At "dinner-time" and "playtime" and "singing in the hall" he pushed Bo the way he had to go, but Bo didn't seem to learn much English from being pushed. England was his home now, but somehow it didn't feel like home to Bo.

So Bo was always pleased when it was Saturday and this Saturday there were strange noises coming from outside. He got up and looked out of the window. Below was the back yard and then a fence and then the empty space, but it wasn't empty now. There were lots of lorries and people shouting and dogs barking. What was going on, Bo wondered.

Father and Mother and Elder Sister worked late at night and were still asleep, so Bo ran downstairs and helped himself to *congee*, rice porridge, and tea. Then he went out to the back yard and stood on a box and looked over the fence. There were tents on the empty space now and a merry-go-round with wooden horses and swings and dodgem cars, and now Bo knew what was going on. It was a fair. He had been to fairs in Hong Kong.

Bo spent most of the morning standing on his box, watching the fair being set up. Charlie was wandering round and watching too.

"You coming to the fair?" said Charlie. Bo shook his head.

"Oh, come on," Charlie said. "I'm your friend, aren't I? I'll look after you."

"Friend?" said Bo, not sure he

188

knew the word. "Can't."

"Why not?" Charlie said. "Ask your father if you can come."

"Can't," said Bo.

"I'll ask him, then," Charlie said, and he ran along the pavement and knocked on the side door of the Ho Ho Take-Away.

"Please," he said, "I'm Bo's friend from Oak Road School. Can Bo come to the fair?"

"Friend?" Father said, and Bo wasn't at all sure Father knew the word either, but suddenly Father smiled. "OK," he said. "Good for son to have friend, good for son to go to fair." And he put a fifty-pence coin into Bo's hands.

"Why do you call it the Ho Ho Take-Away, Mr Lee?" Charlie asked. "It sounds funny in English."

"Ho Ho mean 'excellent' in English," Father said. "What funny?"

"Well, Ho Ho is laughing in English," Charlie tried to explain.

"Laughing Take-Away not OK?" Father said.

"Not OK," said Charlie.

The two boys ran along the pavement. Loud music was coming from the empty space and there were lots of people. The merry-go-round was going round and round and the wooden horses were going up and down.

"Coming on the merry-go-round?" Charlie said, but Bo looked at the silver coin in his hand and shook his head.

"Can't," he said. For a few minutes he watched as Charlie climbed up and got on a wooden horse and then the merry-go-round started.

"Roll up, roll up, four rings to throw for fifty pence!" a man was shouting very loudly, and then Bo noticed the goldfish. Lots of goldfish in a tank. He put his face close to the glass and stared into the greenish water. Back in Hong Kong, Grandfather kept goldfish in a blue and white jar on his bedroom shelf.

"Come along, lad," said the man with the rings. "Four rings for fifty pence and you might win a goldfish."

"OK," said Bo, and he gave the man his money and threw the rings just as he had in Hong Kong and he won a goldfish. The man scooped a goldfish out of the tank with a net and popped it into a plastic bag.

"There you are, then," he said.

"Can . . ." Bo began, but stopped and blinked because he couldn't think of the right words.

"Can what? Speak up, lad," said the man, and just then Charlie ran up.

"Can the fish live in the plastic bag?" said Charlie.

"Of course not," said the man. "Fish need plenty of water. Take it

193

home and put it into something big."

"Can't . . ." Bo began.

"Tell you what," said Charlie, and his freckled face was all excited. "You stop right here and I'll be back very quick. OK?"

"OK," said Bo. He waited, but Charlie didn't come back. He stared at the goldfish in the plastic bag. It swam round ten times, twenty times, a hundred times, and still Charlie hadn't come back. Perhaps Charlie was tired of looking after him, tired of being his friend, Bo thought, and he walked home.

The Ho Ho Take-Away was quiet.

Father and Mother had gone shopping. "Fish need plenty of water," the man had said. Bo went into the kitchen and filled the wok with water and put the goldfish in it. The goldfish swam round and round. You could see it quite liked swimming round and round the wok. But then Father came home.

"The wok is for cooking, son," Father said crossly. "Take that goldfish out."

"Sorry," said Bo, and he popped the goldfish back in the plastic bag and went upstairs to the bathroom. He filled the basin and put the goldfish in. It swam round and round and you could see it quite liked the basin, but then Elder Sister came in.

"I want to wash," she said. "Take that goldfish out."

"Sorry, sorry," said Bo, and he put the goldfish back in the plastic bag. There was a vase on the shelf and he filled it with water and put the goldfish in, but Mother came in.

"Vase is for these flowers, son," Mother said. "Take the goldfish out."

"Sorry, sorry, sorry," Bo said, and he put the goldfish back in the plastic bag and sat down on the stairs.

"Can't . . ." Bo said in a loud

voice. "Fish in bag not OK. Fish need plenty of water. Fish need something big."

Downstairs there was a ring at the side doorbell. Charlie stood on the doorstep with something under his arm. He was very pink and out of breath.

"I ran and ran, but you didn't wait," he said. "I had a goldfish bowl at home but it took ages to find it. It's a goldfish bowl for your goldfish, Bo."

"Thanks," said Bo. He filled the bowl with water and popped the goldfish in. You could tell it liked the bowl very much by the way it swam round and round and round.

Bo carried the goldfish bowl up to his bedroom and put it on the shelf. A blue and white jar like Grandfather had was good, he thought, but a glass goldfish bowl was even better.

The goldfish bowl is still there, and the little goldfish still swims

round and round, and it's the first thing Bo sees when he wakes up. Bo and Charlie are still good friends but Bo knows much more English and he's got quite used to Oak Road School. He still helps Father behind the counter most nights, but now Ho Ho Excellent Take-Away is written over the door.

Carol Singing

Dick King-Smith

Christmas was coming, and one of the teachers was banging away on the piano, as the school practised for the end-of-term service.

"O come, let us adore Him!" sang all one hundred and twenty children.

At any rate one hundred and nineteen of them sang, while the one hundred and twentieth opened her mouth and made a dreadful noise.

"Oh, that voice!" said the headmistress afterwards, as she drank her coffee in the staffroom. "You can hear it above all the rest."

"It's like a cow mooing," said someone.

"No, more like a pig squealing."

"Or a dog howling."

"And to think," said the headmistress, "that when that child was born, her parents chose to call her Carol!"

"It's pathetic really," said Carol's class teacher. "She loves singing."

"Singing, you call it?"

"I mean, she loves music. She knows all the words, of all the carols, Carol does."

"But not the tunes."

"No, I'm afraid she has absolutely no ear for music."

"Unfortunately," said the headmistress, "we each have two ears and Carol's frightful voice is all I can hear. No matter how nicely the other children sing 'I saw three ships come sailing by', all I can hear is that foghorn bellowing its warning of rocks ahead. For goodness' sake, when it comes to the church service, try to get her to keep her voice down."

"Why don't you keep your voice

down?" a catty girl called Catherine was saying to Carol out in the playground.

"I didn't speak," said Carol.

"I don't mean now. I mean when we're singing. You're awful, you are. You're tone deaf."

"What's that mean?" asked Carol.

"It means," said a know-all girl called Noelle, "that you can't tell differences in musical pitch. I've got perfect pitch, I have."

"It sounds all right inside my head," Carol said.

"Well, keep it there," they said. "Don't let it out to give everyone else a headache."

*

It had always been the same. It wasn't too bad when Carol first went to school, because quite a few of the infants weren't all that good at singing in tune. But as time passed and they all grew older, everyone else seemed to get the hang of it. Of course not all of the children had good voices, but they all seemed to rub along all right and those that weren't brilliant at least had the sense to sing softly.

But not Carol. She liked to keep going full blast, and if she ever hit a right note, it was a complete fluke.

The day of the carol service

dawned and Carol's teacher watched anxiously as the children came in through the classroom door. It's not nice of me, she thought, but if only Carol could have a cold today, the kind that makes you lose your voice. But there was no such luck.

"Sing a bit quietly today, Carol, won't you?" the teacher said before they set out.

"Why?"

"Well, you do . . . shout a bit."

But even though the church was full of mums and dads and grandparents and many others as well as all the children, and even though her teacher had put Carol at the very far end of a pew and behind a large pillar, still she could clearly be heard through all the singing.

Some people were amused and smiled, some frowned angrily, several babies burst out crying, and one of the grandfathers

switched off his hearing aid, as, through carol and carol, there sounded the drones and groans and moans of that awful voice.

"It isn't as if she was just a bit sharp or flat," said know-all Noelle afterwards. "She's just absolutely tuneless."

"Oh, I don't know," said catty Catherine. "She wasn't too bad on the Amens," and they went off together, giggling.

Carol walked home alone, wondering for the thousandth time why it was that, though she could hear the tunes clearly in her mind, they came out all wrong.

"I *wish* I could sing properly," she said, and then she had an idea.

"Why shouldn't I be taught?" she said. "After all, you can be taught anything – how to read, how to write, how to do sums, and later on things like how to drive a car. Why can't you be taught to sing?"

So as soon as she got home, she opened the Yellow Pages.

SINGING TUITION (she found)
see MUSIC TEACHERS

There were several names under this heading, and one was in the very next street to hers. She went to find her mother.

"Mum," she said. "Can I have

singing lessons?"

"Why?" said Carol's mother. What's the use, she thought.

"I just want to learn to sing in tune, that's all. I can hear the music in my head, but when I open my mouth, it comes out all funny."

"I know, dear."

"And look, there's a music teacher in the next street, Mum," said Carol, and she pointed to the place in the Yellow Pages.

"Who's going to pay for these lessons?" asked her mother.

"Me. I'll save up. Honest. Can I have them? Please?"

"We'd better go and see," said Carol's mother.

So next morning, a Saturday, they went together to a little house in the next street and knocked on the door. On it was a notice

MISS N. CHANTER
MUSIC TEACHER

It was opened by a little old lady with grey hair done in a bun and the nicest, smiliest sort of face.

"Hello," she said. "What can I do for you?"

"My daughter wants singing lessons," said Carol's mother. "How much do you charge?"

"That depends," said Miss N. Chanter. "Come in, and we'll see."

She led them into a small room mostly filled by a large piano, on top of which a black cat lay sleeping.

Miss N. Chanter sat down at the piano.

"Now then," she said, "what's your name?"

"Carol."

"Hm. Do you like music?"

"Oh yes! I like all sorts of music and I know loads of different tunes. I can hear them all in my head perfectly, but when I open my mouth they don't come out quite right. I just want to be able to sing properly, like everyone else at school."

"Well, let's try," said Miss N. Chanter, and she played the first few bars of "God save the Queen".

"Know the words?" she said.

"Oh yes!"

"OK. Let's go. One . . . two . . ."

"Well, well," said Miss N. Chanter after the last quavering "Queen" had died away and the black cat had dashed from the room with all his fur standing on end, "I see what you mean, Carol. Or rather I hear what you mean. We have problems."

"You mean you can't teach me?" said Carol.

"I didn't say that."

"You mean it's going to cost a lot

212

of money?" said Carol's mother.

"I didn't say that either. In fact, if I can't teach Carol to sing, I won't charge you a penny."

That's all right then, thought Carol's mother, she hasn't got a hope.

So they fixed that Carol should come by herself for her first lesson in a week's time.

"I've had an idea!" was the first thing Miss N. Chanter said when she opened the door to Carol on the next Saturday morning. "I believe you when you say you can hear tunes in your head but it's what comes out of your mouth that's the

213

trouble. Now, if we could catch the tunes on their way out . . ."

"I don't understand," said Carol.

Miss N. Chanter put her hand in the pocket of her woolly cardigan and took out a small mouth-organ. She held it out to Carol.

"Try this," she said.

"But I can't play any instrument," said Carol.

"This isn't just any instrument. Try playing a tune on it. Low notes on the left, high notes on the right. All you've got to do is blow and suck. Go on."

Carol hesitated. This is silly, she thought, I've never played a mouth-organ before. It will just be a horrid noise, and, as though she had spoken out loud, Miss N. Chanter said, "No, it won't. Choose something simple, a nursery rhyme, say. How about 'Pop Goes the Weasel', know the tune of that? Right then, just sing it in your head and suck and blow."

Just what it was that made her move the mouth-organ to left or to right or told her when to suck and when to blow Carol never could afterwards understand. But she never forgot the playing of that first simple little tune. Every note was right. No one could have played "Pop Goes the Weasel" better. Even the black cat purred loudly.

"I thought as much," said Miss N. Chanter. "It's just a question of catching the melody that's in your head before it gets out into the open air. Now choose another tune."

So Carol chose "Widecombe Fair" and the tune came out perfectly, every bit of it, old Uncle Tom Cobley and all!

Carol took the mouth-organ out of her mouth and stared at it in wonder.

"It's magic!" she said.

"You could say that," said Miss N. Chanter.

216

"It's wonderful," said Carol, "but . . ."

"But what?"

". . . but how will it teach me to sing?"

Miss N. Chanter sat down at the piano and played the scale of C Major.

Then with one finger she struck middle C.

"Play that," she said.

Carol played it.

"Now this time," said Miss N. Chanter, "I'll hit the note again, you play it, and then quickly take the thing out of your mouth and sing it – 'Lah'."

And it worked! Carol sang the

perfect middle C!

After that it was plain sailing.

At the second lesson Carol
could play a scale on the mouth-
organ and then she was managing
without the mouth-organ,
singing to Miss N. Chanter's
accompaniment on the piano,
and by the end of the tenth
lesson she could sing any tune
unaccompanied.

"That's it, then, Carol," said
Miss N. Chanter. "You can sing.
And what's more, you've a very
good voice."

"It's all thanks to you and your
mouth-organ," said Carol. "Please,
how much do I owe you?"

"Oh, we'll see about that," said Miss N. Chanter. "Now let's have one last song. How about 'Over the Rainbow'? D'you know that?"

"Oh yes!" cried Carol. "How funny you should choose that! We're going to do *The Wizard of Oz* for the school concert this term."

"Fancy!" said Miss N. Chanter. "Tell you what, Carol, if you get the part of Dorothy, I won't charge you a penny."

"Who's going to play Dorothy?" said the headmistress to the teacher who was organising the concert.

219

"Oh, Noelle, I should think," said the teacher. "She's got perfect pitch and not a bad voice. There are a number of girls who might be good enough. I'll have an audition."

"Don't bother with Carol," the headmistress said, and everybody laughed.

You can guess the rest, can't you?

Half a dozen girls tried for the part of Dorothy, and know-all Noelle was maybe the best. But before she could be told so, one more girl had come into the room.

"What are you doing here, Carol?" the teacher said. "We're

auditioning for *The Wizard of Oz*, you know."

"She could make the noises for the Cowardly Lion," said catty Catherine, and the others sniggered.

"Please," said Carol. "I want to be Dorothy."

"Carol must have the part beyond the shadow of a doubt," said the teacher to the headmistress afterwards. "She put me in mind of the young Judy Garland. She sang 'Over the Rainbow' quite beautifully. She'll bring the house down!"

"I cannot understand it," said

the headmistress. "It smacks of witchcraft."

And you won't be surprised to hear that, at the end of the school concert, among the clapping, cheering audience that stood to applaud the wonderful singing of Carol as Dorothy in *The Wizard of*

Oz was a little old lady with grey hair done in a bun and the nicest, smiliest sort of face.

ACKNOWLEDGEMENTS

The publishers wish to thank the following for permission to reproduce copyright material:

Joan Aiken: for "Tale of a One-Way Street" from *A Tale of a One-Way Street and Other Stories* by Joan Aiken, first published by Jonathan Cape (1978). Copyright © Joan Aiken Enterprises Ltd, 1978, reproduced by permission of A M Heath & Co Ltd on behalf of the author.

Malorie Blackman: for "Betsey and the Mighty Marble" from *Betsey Bigalow*, first published by Piccadilly Press. Copyright © Malorie Blackman, reproduced by permission of The Agency (London) Ltd on behalf of the author.

Barbee Oliver Carleton: for "The Pretend Pony" from *More Bedtime Stories to Read*, first published by Golden Pleasure Books (1963), reproduced by permission of the author.

Adèle Geras: for "A Zebra for Helen" from *Apricots at Midnight* by Adèle Geras, first published by Hamish Hamilton (1977). Copyright © Adèle Geras 1977, reproduced by permission of Laura Cecil Literary Agency on behalf of the author.

Margaret Joy: for "Mr Gill Makes a Wish" from *Allotment Lane School* by Margaret Joy, first published by Faber and Faber (1985), reproduced by permission of Faber and Faber Ltd.

Geraldine Kaye: from "The Little Goldfish" first published in *Tobie and the Face Merchant and Other Stories for Six-Year-Olds* first published by HarperCollins Publishers (1991). Copyright © Geraldine Kaye 1991, reproduced by permission of A M Heath & Co Ltd on behalf of the author.

Dick King-Smith: for "Carol Singing" from *Philibert the First* by Dick King-Smith, first published by Viking (1994); and "Fat Lawrence" from *Animal Stories* by Dick King-Smith, first published by Viking (1997), reproduced by permission of A P Watt Ltd on behalf of Fox Busters Ltd.

Rudyard Kipling: for "How The Whale Got His Throat" from *Just So Stories* by Rudyard Kipling, reproduced by permission of A P Watt Ltd on behalf of The National Trust for Places of Historical Interest or Natural Beauty.

Margaret Mahy: for "Elephant Milk, Hippopotamus Cheese" from *The Downhill Crocodile Whizz and Other Stories*, first published by J M Dent, reproduced by permission of The Orion Publishing Group Ltd.

ACKNOWLEDGEMENTS

Pat Thomson: for "Hair of a Cat" from *Snakes on the Bus and Other Pet Stories*, ed. Valerie Bierman, first published by Methuen Children's Books (1994). Copyright © 1994 Pat Thomson, reproduced by permission of Laura Cecil Literary Agency on behalf of the author.

Every effort has been made to trace the copyright holders but where this has not been possible or where any error has been made the publishers will be pleased to make the necessary arrangement at the first opportunity.

Animal stories

for **6** year olds

Chosen by Helen Paiba

A bright and varied selection of
heart-warming animal stories by some
of the very best writers for children.
Perfect for reading alone or aloud – and for
dipping into time and time again.
With stories from David Henry Wilson,
Meredith Hooper, Dick King-Smith,
Margaret Mahy and many more, this book
will provide hours of fantastic fun.

Funny stories

for 6 year olds

Chosen by Helen Paiba

A bright and varied selection of wonderfully
entertaining stories by some of the very
best writers for children. Perfect for
reading alone or aloud — and for dipping
into time and time again. With stories from
Margaret Mahy, David Henry Wilson, Francesca
Simon, Tony Bradman and many more,
this book will provide hours of fantastic fun.

Magical Stories

Chosen by Helen Paiba

A bright and varied selection of marvellously magical stories by some of the very best writers for children. Perfect for reading alone or aloud – and for dipping into time and time again. With stories from the Brothers Grimm, Berlie Doherty, Joan Aiken, Geraldine McCaughrean and many more, this book will provide hours of fantastic fun.

Funny stories

for 7 Year Olds

Chosen by Helen Paiba

A bright and varied selection of wonderfully entertaining stories by some of the very best writers for children. Perfect for reading alone or aloud — and for dipping into time and time again. With stories from Dick King-Smith, Michael Bond, Philippa Gregory, Jacqueline Wilson and many more, this book will provide hours of fantastic fun.

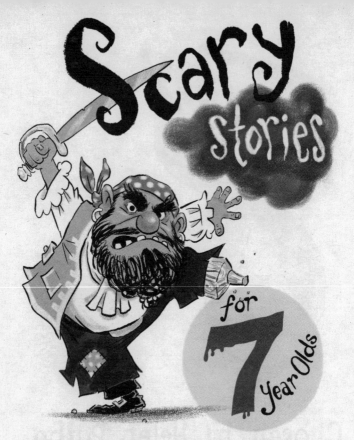

Scary stories

for 7 Year Olds

Chosen by Helen Paiba

A bright and varied selection of hair-raisingly
scary stories by some of the very best
writers for children. Perfect for reading
alone or aloud – and for dipping into time and
time again. With stories from Michael Rosen,
Catherine Storr, Jamie Rix, Rose Impey
and many more, this book will provide
hours of fantastic fun.